For Kasia
A.J.B.

To duck lovers
Irene and Cesare
F.C.

Text copyright © Alan James Brown 2010
Illustrations copyright © Francesca Chessa 2010
First published in Great Britain in 2010 by Gullane Children's Books
185 Fleet Street, London EC4A 2HS
First published in the United States of America by Holiday House, Inc. in 2010
All Rights Reserved
HOLIDAY HOUSE is registered in the U. S. Patent and Trademark Office.
Printed and Bound in November 2009 in Chachoengsao, Thailand, at Sirivatana Interprint Public Co., Ltd.
www.holidayhouse.com
First American Edition
1 3 5 7 9 10 8 6 4 2
Library of Congress Cataloging-in-Publication Data
Brown, Alan James.
Love-a-duck / by Alan James Brown ; illustrated by Francesca Chessa.—1st American ed.
p. cm.
Summary: After falling out of the window and spending an unforgettable day outdoors,
a plastic duck is returned home safely, just in time for little Jane's bath.
ISBN 978-0-8234-2263-0 (hardcover)
[1. Toys—Fiction. 2. Ducks—Fiction.] I. Chessa, Francesca, ill. II. Title.
PZ7.B81268Lo 2010
[E]—dc22
2009029940

Love-a-Duck

by Alan James Brown

illustrated by Francesca Chessa

Holiday House / New York

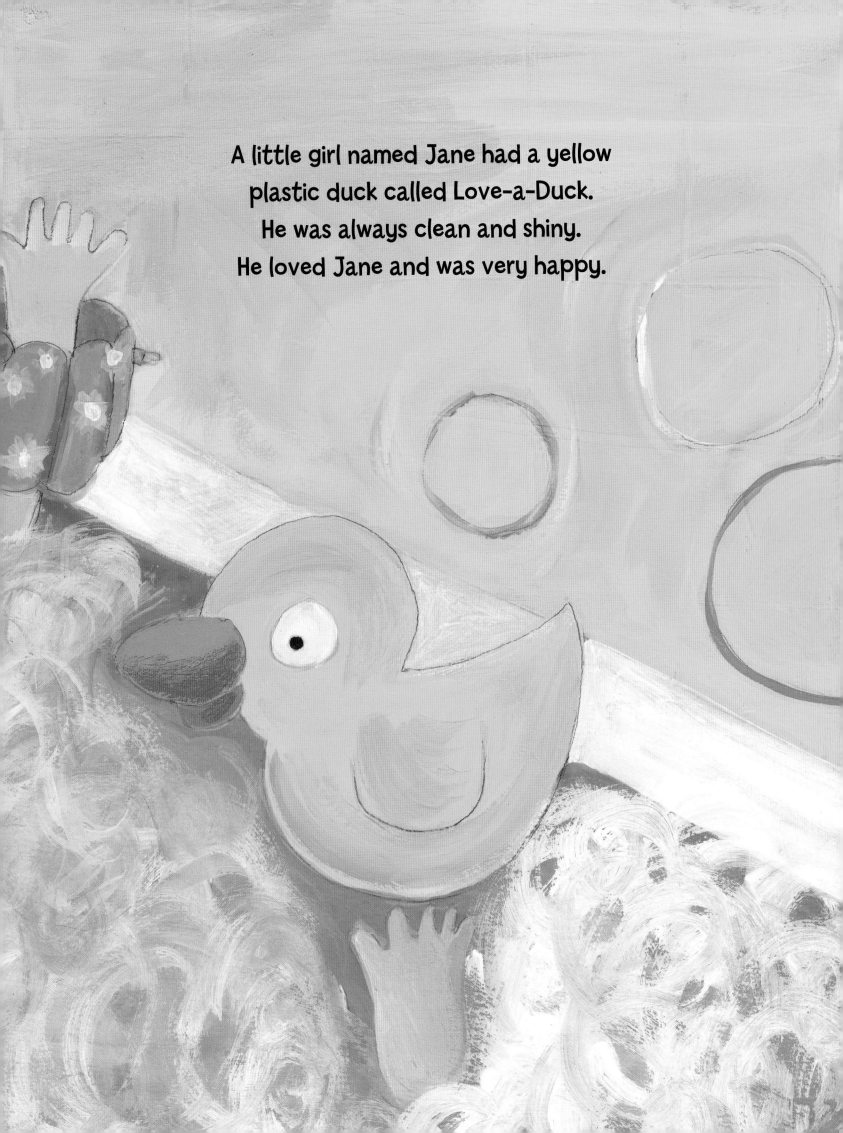

A little girl named Jane had a yellow
plastic duck called Love-a-Duck.
He was always clean and shiny.
He loved Jane and was very happy.

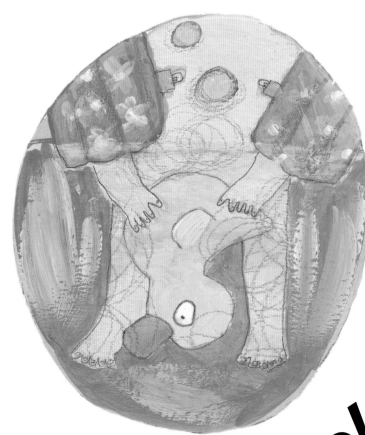

Jane pushed Love-a-Duck under
the water and let him bounce up. . . .

BOING!

She squeezed soapy water out of him. Love-a-Duck tried to squeak, but all he could say was . . .

"**Squirt, Squirt!**"

"Oh, Love-a-Duck!" said Jane. "You can't even squeak!" Love-a-Duck felt very sad. He thought that Jane didn't love him anymore.

Mom put Love-a-Duck on the windowsill
while she cleaned the bathtub. He was so full of water
that he toppled over and fell out of the window.
Did anybody see?

No, they didn't!

Love-a-Duck landed in . . .

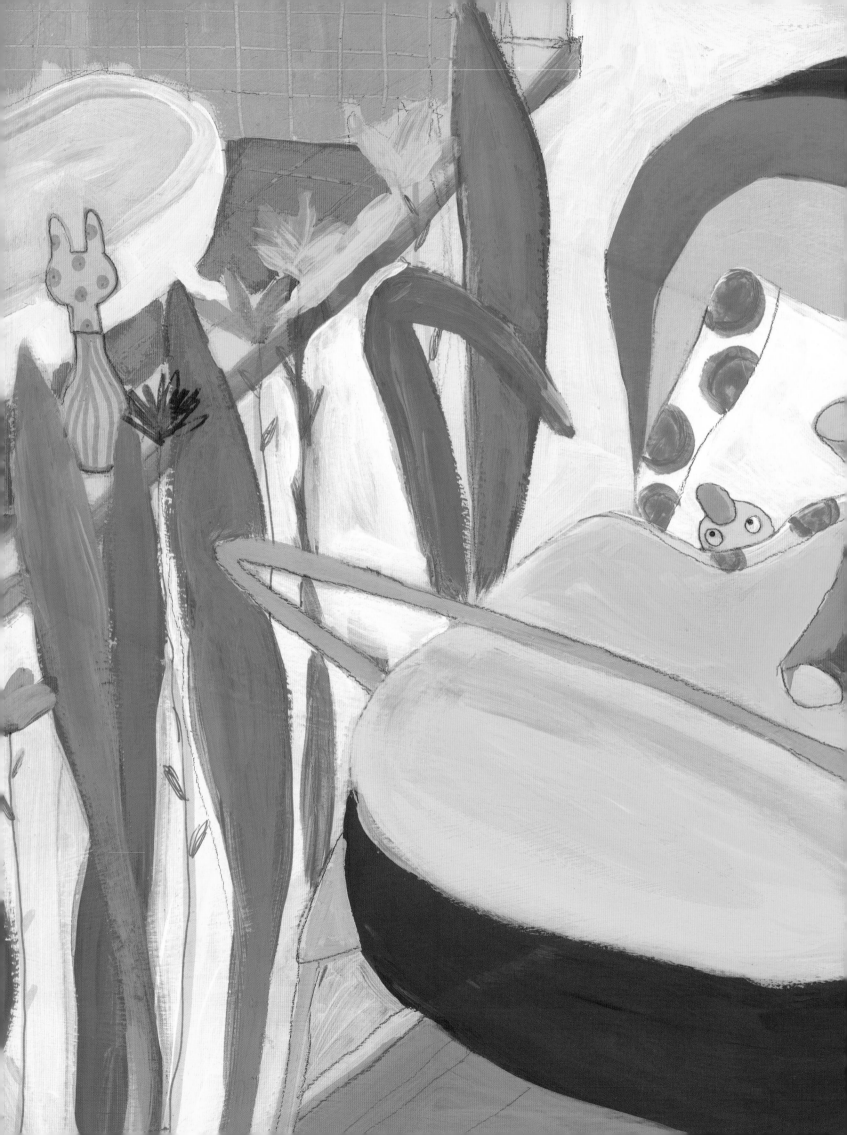

John's carriage.

Love-a-Duck wanted
to get out of the carriage.
He tried to squeak, but
all he could say was . . .

"Squidge, Squidge!"

Mom, Jane, and John came out with Buster the dog,
and together they started down the road.
Did anybody know that Love-a-Duck was in the carriage with John?

No, they didn't!

At the park, Jane played
on the swings. Mom lifted
John out of the carriage
and Love-a-Duck
fell out . . .
and then . . .

Buster the dog grabbed
him and ran away.
Did anybody see?

No, they didn't!

All the bathwater was squeezed out
of Love-a-Duck. He tried to squeak,
but all he could say was . . .

"Squoo, Squoo!"

Buster saw the ducks on the pond.
He opened his jaws to bark, and
Love-a-Duck fell into the water.
Did anybody see?

No, they didn't!

The wind blew Love-a-Duck across the pond

He thought he was swimming, like a real duck.

Love-a-Duck tried to squeak, but all he could say was . . .

"Squark, Squark!"

Was he turning into a real duck?

"Real ducks dabble in the mud,"
said the ducks, and they splashed Love-a-Duck with mud.
He tried to squeak, but all he could say was . . .
"Squish, Squish!"

The ducks laughed at Love-a-Duck and flew away.
Love-a-Duck tried to fly, but his wings didn't work.
He was stuck in the middle of the pond—
and felt very sad.

Love-a-Duck tried to swim,
but he just turned upside down in the
water. And as a fish pushed him back
to the side of the pond, he tried to
squeak, but all he could say was . . .

"Squubble, Squubble!"

Jane was at the
top of the slide.
Did she see him?

No, she didn't!

"Time to go home!" said Mom.
Would anyone ever
see Love-a-Duck?

Yes! At last
somebody saw him.

Buster the dog grabbed Love-a-Duck
and carried him out of
the park following Mom and Jane.
Love-a-Duck tried to squeak,
but all he could say was . . .

"**Squoo, Squoo!**"

At home Mom said, "Hot baths for everyone!"
Jane sat at one end of the bathtub and John at the other,
then Buster put his head over the side and . . .

Love-a-Duck fell into the water!
At once he was clean and shiny again.
Did Jane see him?

Yes, this time . . . she did!

"Love-a-Duck!" said Jane. "You're my best toy!"

Love-a-Duck was so happy!

He loved Jane, and he loved being her toy.

Jane pushed Love-a-Duck under the water.

She let him go and he bounced up.

BOING!

Jane squeezed him.

Loud and clear, Love-a-Duck said . . .

"Squeak, squeak!"